One Day at a Time

Written by Lori Lumley

Illustrated by Marianne Pfaeffli

Balboa Press books may be ordered through booksellers or by contacting:

Balboa Press
A Division of Hay House
1663 Liberty Drive
Bloomington, IN 47403
www.balboapress.com
1 (877) 407-4847

ISBN: 978-1-9822-1182-0 (sc)
ISBN: 978-1-9822-1181-3 (e)

Library of Congress Control Number: 2018910066

Print information available on the last page.

Balboa Press rev. date: 09/07/2018

BALBOA.
PRESS
A DIVISION OF HAY HOUSE

Dedicated to
Cayden & Carissa

One day –
You were born
and my heart became bigger

The next day —
I held you
Until we both fell asleep in
Peaceful dreams

Everyday –
You inspire me

One day –
I watched you sing in front of a
crowd of people
and my heart sang too

Another day –
You lost someone you loved
and together we cried

Every passing day –
You grow

Everyday –
You change a little more

Some days —
I see myself in you

Most days –
I marvel at who you have become
You are a miracle

God created you –
You are wonderfully divine

I have never been more blessed —
knowing you are mine

I will love you forever
one day at a time

CPSIA information can be obtained
at www.ICGtesting.com
Printed in the USA
BVHW021559211218
536178BV00008B/136/P

9 781982 211820